Andrew Downing

The Trumpeters

and other poems - Vol. 1

Andrew Downing

The Trumpeters
and other poems - Vol. 1

ISBN/EAN: 9783337314941

Printed in Europe, USA, Canada, Australia, Japan

Cover: Foto ©Andreas Hilbeck / pixelio.de

More available books at **www.hansebooks.com**

THE TRUMPETERS,

AND

OTHER POEMS.

BY

ANDREW DOWNING.

If my best food mislikes your taste,

And my best wine provokes your frown,

Then tarry not with me, but haste,—

For there are other inns in town.

Thomas Bailey Aldrich.

HAYWORTH PUBLISHING HOUSE:
WASHINGTON, D. C.
1897.

INDEX.

	Page
The Trumpeters	9
Gretchen's Baby	11
Vi Et Armis	15
Twilight	16
The Dreamer	17
Omnipotence	21
The Sphinx	22
Fame	24
Her Amulet	25
When Love Came Back	26
The Violin	27
Life's Common Things	28
Ich Dien	29
Scotland and the Scots	30
The Dew	32
Your Enemy	33
My Sailor Lad	34
Now	35
Beyond the Sunset Hills	36
From the Persian	37
Semper Idem	38

	Page
Counterparts	39
A Brighter Morrow	40
The Rose of the Prairie	42
The Humming-Bird	44
The Dells	45
The Oriole	47
Leonore	48
In Revery	49
Ben Murad	50
Eve at Mt. Taconia	51
Robert Burns	52
The Sweetest Song	54
The Blue-Bird	56
October's Amber Days	58
My Saint	60
Our Daily Bread	61
Among the Roses	63
Dementia	64
The Daisy in the South	65
John Ericsson	67
Dandelions	69
The Poet	70
The Green and Gold	76
The Red Bird	77
Aspiration	78
Memorial Day	79
Golden Rod	81
Auf Wiedersehen	82
Christine	83
At the Seaside	84

	Page
To Estelle	85
The Wheat Harvest	87
Keep Sunshine in the Heart	91
Moonrise	92
The Sweetest Rose	93
A Picture	94
Deacon Pettibone	97
A Summer Night	99
Ship from Fortune's Isle	101
The Heart will Remember	103
The Bells of Brookline	105
To Minnie	107
The Rose She Wore	108
The Better Day	109
An Idyl	111
Child-Questionings	113
The Lady Moon	114
Destiny	115
The Ideal Farmer	117
The Old and the New	120
Thanksgiving	122
The President Lives	125
Hesperus	127
Companionship	128
October	129
The Optimist	131
Winter Birds	132
The Spanish Love Song	134
Morning Hymn	135
The Pioneers	136

The Trumpeters.

The winds of March are trumpeters,
  They blow with might and main,
And herald to the waiting earth
  The Spring, and all her train.

They harbinger the April showers,
  With sunny smiles between,
That wake the blossoms in their beds,
  And make the meadows green.

The south will send her spicy breath,
  The brook in music flow,
The orchard don a bloomy robe
  Of May's unmelting snow.

9

Then June will stretch her golden days,
  Like harp-strings, bright and long,
And play a rich accompaniment
  To every wild bird's song.

The fair midsummer-time, apace,
  Shall bring us many a boon,
And ripened fruits, and yellow sheaves,
  Beneath the harvest-moon.

The golden-rod, a Grecian torch,
  Will light the splendid scene,
When Autumn comes in all the pomp
  And glory of a queen.

Her crimson sign shall flash and shine
  On every wooded hill,
And Plenty's horn unto the brim
  Her lavish bounty fill.

Then, little sweetheart, murmur not,
  Nor shrug your shoulders so;
The winds of March are trumpeters,—
  I love to hear them blow.

GRETCHEN'S BABY.

Heinrich is my nearest neighbor—there he lives, across
    the way.
Gretchen toils beside her husband, in the meadow day
    by day,
Leaving little Heinrich playing in the frowzy, fragrant
    hay.

In the shadow of a maple, where the gipsy winds ap-
    pear—
Whispering the sylvan secrets that the winds, alone, may
    hear—
Lies the baby, unattended, neither maid nor matron near.

Passing through the ancient orchard, with my fishing-
    rods and reels
Suddenly I come upon him, as he elevates his heels,—
And I smile to note the pleasure that the little Teuton
    feels.

Blooms of two brief summers, only, on his pathway have
   been cast,
But the feet of many sunbeams in his curls are tangled
   fast,
And his eyes are blue as heaven—when the storm is
   overpast.
All the strange confusion round him comes to his bewild-
   ered ken,—
Stalk and stubble, blade and blossom, and a green leaf
   now and then—
Crossed, and variant and chaotic, as the purposes of
   men.

Now the red-caps of the clover in the windrows have a
   claim
On the lilliput's attention, and he reaches for the
   same,
Eagerly, and turns them over, wondering from whence
   they came.

Now he spies that frail creation, a bedizened butterfly,
Circling round him in the sunshine, mounting airily on
   high,—
As it were a splendid blossom, winged, and floating in
   the sky.

Is the little fellow conscious, as the sunshine warms the
    west,
That the evening hour approaches, bringing him its per-
    fect rest,—
Folded in the white asylum of the gentle mother-
    breast?

Now the twain are coming toward him, in the twilight
    dim and gray,
Stopping once to give him signal, just a moment, on the
    way,
And he leaps as if to meet them, smiling like a cherub
    gay.

I reflect, and I remember that betimes, in Nature's plan,
Smallest parcels are the richest—so perhaps this midget-
    man
May enfold a germ of greatness rare since Time his march
    began.

And I ask the woman questions of the old home by the
    Rhine,
And uncover with another what would seem a deep
    design:
"Would you sell your baby, Gretchen?" But she laughs,
    and answers, "*Nein!*"

I should get, through such a purchase, not alone poor
    Heinrich's son,
But Germanic strength and valor, with a magazine of
    fun,
And a storage-house of patience, and contentment, all in
    one.

Happy father, child and mother! Picture exquisite and
    sweet!
Chain by Love securely welded—triple links, and all
    complete;
Wanting one, would life be fairer, though the world were
    at their feet?

All the laureates of England who have lived since
    Chaucer's day,
Never wrote so grand a poem, never sang so sweet a lay
As your poem-baby, Gretchen, playing in the scented
    hay!

VI ET ARMIS.

'Tis an ancient Roman proverb:
  "Whoso braveth desp'rate odds,
Wins the potent stars to aid him,
  And the favor of the gods!"

Every brave and strong endeavor
  Helps heroic souls to rise
Unto higher heights of triumph—
  Nearer to the smiling skies.

Life is but a broad arena—
  But a mighty contest-ring,
And the struggle, to the victor,
  Doth a glorious guerdon bring.

Be the prize you seek, my brother,
  Where the battle-banners flame,
Knowledge, wisdom, hand of woman,
  Power, or station, wealth, or fame,

Be the first to join the onset,
  Though you traverse flood and fire;
Smite, relentless, every foeman
  That would foil your soul's desire.

Knightly faith, and Roman courage,
  Live, and hold the vantage still;
Valor wins the victor's garland—
  You can conquer if you will!

TWILIGHT.

As a sweet, silent nun, to vespers going,
  The shadowy Twilight steals across the land—
Her somber robes about her softly flowing—
  And from her rosary, at Love's command,
Tells dewy beads, the shining pearls bestowing
  On leaf, and flower, with rev'rent, tender hand.

THE DREAMER.

By the "Gate Beautiful," that leads
To song-land, and its flow'ry meads—
Where all the deeper glories lie,
Of earth and air, of sea and sky—
In lone estate, dream-tranced, I wait
From early morn to even late;
And, waiting, make demand from all
That come my way—a tribute small.

Unto the soaring bird I say:
Trill me your sweetest roundelay;
And to the fire-fly in the dark:
Illume my pathway with your spark;
And to the honey-laden bee:
Divide your store of sweets with me;
And to the breeze that comes and goes:
Bring me the perfume of the rose;
And to the bright sun rolling high:
Paint me a rainbow on the sky;

And to the sea-waves on the beach:
To me your wordless anthem teach;
And to the river, deep and wide:
Lend me the calmness of your tide.
Give me your song, O whippoorwill!
Complaining from the wooded hill;
And I would hear, when day declines,
The organ-music of the pines—
The harps aeolian in trees,
And all celestial harmonies
That fall in cadence, sweet and clear,
And touch the inner, spirit ear.

O'ermastered by insatiate greed,
With my good angel, too, I plead:
Show me all fair and glorious sights
That bless the days, and cheer the nights—
The sun-burst from the cloudy bars—
The solemn beauty of the stars;
Mirage, whose potent magic frets
The sky with domes, and minarets;
The tall sierra-peaks that stand
As warders of a mighty land;
The summer sky's serenest blue—

The glory of a globe of dew;
All wild and wide Sahara-tracts,
And mist-hung, roaring cataracts;
And golden lands of fruits and flowers,
Whose blossoms tell the passing hours—
Whose purple grapes outvie the store
The burdened vines of Eschol bore.

Show me the stately monarch-trees
In all the world's Yo-Semites;
Cathedrals, palaces, and towers,
In other lands, remote from ours;
The grand old painters' works sublime,
By gen'rous Art bequeathed to Time;
The world wherein the sculptor dwells,
And all is marble miracles.

Bring near those souls, those comrade-friends
With whom my soul in sweetness blends;
Fair Childhood, with its merry laugh,
And Old Age leaning on his staff;
And lusty Manhood, sun-embrowned,
And Womanhood with glory crowned;
And Love, and Friendship—royal pair—
That make all climes, all seasons fair.

All joys, all sorrows, I would gauge
That are the common heritage;
All thoughts, all feelings, all delights,
That sound the depths, or touch the heights—
That stir the deeps of soul, or sense,
In all life's wide experience.

And, holding treasures rare as these,
And keys of many mysteries,
Mayhap the dreamer shall not wait
Expectant long—before the gate,
But enter in with small delay—
Behold the fabled fountains play,
And tread the flower-enameled meads,
And blow his pipe of slender reeds.

And, if he may not sound, perchance,
Such notes as made the forests dance
In eld, upon the Grecian plains,
Allured by Orpheus' melting strains—
Nor help the weary world along
With new delights of joy and song—
His art with tenderness may touch
Some hearts that sorrow overmuch;

He may some modest offering lay
On Love's sweet altar, day by day;
Some little bud of richer hope
His hand may nurture, that will ope
In blossom, 'neath the summer sky,
And shed its fragrance—bye-and-bye.

OMNIPOTENCE.

God writes his autograph in starry script
  Upon the fair, blue tablet of the sky;
    So, too, the wondrous cloud-ships, sailing by—
That, late, in some far port, their moorings slipped—
Whose snowy sails and pennons have been dipped
    In sunset seas, and stained with crimson dye—
    Proclaim the majesty of Him on high!
The modest, woodland blossom, honey-lipped,
The dimpling lake, that wild birds sing to sleep,
    The whispering winds in every leafy branch,
      The butterfly, with painted wings unfurled,
Reveal His power,—as when His lightnings leap
    From cloud to cloud; or when His avalanche,
      Flung down an Alp, with thunder shakes the world!

THE SPHINX.

There is in Egypt, near the Pyramids,
Fronting the placid Nile, a monolith,—
A sculptured legacy from aeons, old
Ere yet the Pharoahs lived, or Carthage was,
Or Caesar wore the purple.

                Grim and vast,
In hermit loneliness, it sits and broods
Above the Nubian desert.   Its dull eyes,
Stony and lidless, stare across the sands;
And the colossal, parted, marble lips
Are marble-mute and marble-cold, as when
The gnawing chisel of the sculptor wrought
Their curving outlines; and they answer not
The immemorial question: "What art thou?"

Its origin, or meaning, no man knows;
Inscription there is none, nor hieroglyph,
On wood, or stone, or gray papyrus-roll,
In all the mouldy crypts, and mummy cells,

And buried temples of the antique world,—
Nor any word of Chaldean seer, or sage,
That ever may the mystery unfold.

So, fronting every man that lives, there is
A dark enigma that he may not solve,—
A mute and stony Sphinx whose riddle deep
Is never wholly guessed, though all the lore,
And wisdom of the ages, help the quest.

It is the Future, wide and limitless,
Of life that is, and that which is to be.

Whence came we? Whither do our footsteps tend?
And what shall be the life that follows this
When we shall pass beyond the sunset hills
Into the land of shadows? Who can make
Unto himself an answer,—honest, true,
Sufficient, not conjectural alone?
The unreturning dead send back no word
Of greeting from that unseen, distant world,
Nor babble of its secrets.

                    It is Faith
Alone, that gives us aught of warrant here
To wear the badge of Immortality.

And Faith, not Knowledge, builds for every man,
In his own spiritual consciousness,
The ultimate, bright Heaven of his hope
The realm of joy, the goal of his desire.
No weaker hand can lead the errant soul
From Doubt's dark labyrinth into the light,
And up the starry heights whereon is God.
All else,—amid the strife of sects diverse,
The ceaseless dissonance of warring creeds,
The blight of superstitions, centuries old,—
Is vain—uncertain as the shifting sands
That drift forever round the rocky base
Of that old image on the Gizeh plain.

FAME.

Man toils, and strives, and wastes his little life to claim,—
At last the transient glory of a splendid name,
And have, perchance, in marble mockery a bust,
Poised on a pedestal, above his sleeping dust.

HER AMULET.

Her amulet with gems is bright,
A sapphire blue, a diamond white,
  A charming ruby, rich and warm!
  It shields the lovely maid from harm,
And brings her pleasant dreams at night!

It makes the cloud of sorrow light,
That else her sky would darken quite,
  And checks her tears, and lulls alarm—
          Her amulet!

She deems that Cupid 'twill affright,—
But, oh! she's never met the wight,
  Or she would own how weak the charm
  She wears upon her dimpled arm,
To stay his arrows in their flight—
          Her amulet!

WHEN LOVE CAME BACK.

Young Love was such a torment
    I hid from him my face,
And scorned, and drove him from me
    In bitter, deep disgrace.
He fled my primrose garden,
    His heart was wounded sore,—
I heard him moan, in undertone:
    "I will return no more!"

But Love his vow repented,
    And came, reluctant, back;
I think somebody led him
    Along the primrose track;
His face was at my lattice,
    His cheek was white and thin;
He spoke in such a pleading way
    I could but let him in.

Now Love is such a comfort
I would not have him go
For all the shining treasures
That Fortune can bestow.
And, since his sweet returning,
I bless, with grateful sense,
The day he came, the way he came,
The hand that led him hence.

THE VIOLIN.

A rare violin—'twas an old Stradivarius—
Was broken and mended, a dozen times o'er,
But, touched by the hand of a master, its music
Was richer and sweeter than ever before.

So, often, the heart that is broken by sorrow,
Or wounded by malice, betrayal or wrong,
Is purer thereafter, and wiser and stronger,
And utters a sweeter and tenderer song.

LIFE'S COMMON THINGS.

The common things of life are best,—
   The air, the sun, the rain;
They come and go without our quest—
   They go, and come again.

And treasures in our hands we hold
   That riches cannot buy,
Though there be bags of yellow gold
   Enough to fill the sky.

For us the robin trills his song,
   The oriole pipes his lay,—
A concert all the summer long,
   And not a cent to pay.

And Love's and Friendship's joys are ours,
   And sweet content, and health—
Not always found to be the dowers
   Of luxury and wealth.

The crown of care on greatness pressed,
  May well the soul appall;
The common things of life are best,
  And, dear, we have them all.

≋≋≋≋●≋≋≋≋

ICH DIEN.

I like that motto of the German knight,
  In olden days, embossed upon his shield:
  "Ich Dien!" I see him on the battle field,
A strong, dark-bearded man, in armour bright,—
A swift blade flashing where he leads the fight—
  Erect, self-poised, not all his power revealed,
  Of iron will that doth not bend, nor yield,
Nor turn in stress of danger, left, or right,
Till knightly service wrought hath gained the meed
  Of royal favor, and the world's applause,
    With star, or garter, or the signet-ring.
So every man, by worthy word, or deed,
  A knight may be,—may serve some noble cause,
    And win a jeweled token from The King!

SCOTLAND AND THE SCOTS.

For the anniversary of the birthday of Robert Burns, Jan. 25, 1894.

I know not in what land thy children, O Scotland,
   Remember not proudly the place of their birth;
Brave sons and fair daughters, though over the waters
   They wander afar to the ends of the earth!

Thy fame and thy glory, in ballad and story,
   Are sung and rehearsed, where a Scottish heart beats;
And that flower, good humor, is still a free bloomer
   Whenever, wherever a Scottish clan meets.

And here's a "clan-meeting!" we tender our greeting;
   We welcome you all in the broad-prairied west,—
Scotch fathers and mothers, lads, lassies,—your brothers
   And cousins are we, and we'll give you our best!

To-day is Rob's birthday; we'll make it a mirthday
   Far into the night when the stars are above;
With voices clear-ringing, his sweetest songs singing,—
   The bard of "Auld Scotia," the poet we love!

Through him, Caledonia, all peoples have known ye—
　Through him and the heroes who brighten your fame;
And ever a pressing and lusty "Scotch blessing"
　Shall follow the craven who slanders your name!

O, brave northern nation! you honor each station
　In life through your sons, be it humble, or great;
You send us good teachers, sound lawyers and preachers,
　And statesmen alive to the weal of the state!

In science and letters, we're greatly your debtors;
　In morals, philosophy, learning and art,
Scotch pluck and persistence have bettered existence,
　And broadened the pathway, or furnished the chart!

When "Uncle Sam" wanted a hero undaunted,
　On victory's summit his standard to plant,
A Scot of the border, some chieftain, or warder,
　Leaped forth in the blood of the valorous Grant!

And aye when the rattle, and tumult of battle
　Are heard in the land—with a soul undismayed—
Will Sandy be in it, to stay, and to win it—
　In war, or in politics, law, love or trade!

THE DEW.

I walk at morn where fairies brew,
On moonlit nights the clear, bright dew;
And every blossom holdeth up
In modest grace a dainty cup,
Enwreathed about with glossy leaves;
And every cup a drop receives,
And all the leaves with open palms—
Like little beggars asking alms—
Take the sweet gift with gratitude,
And seem to whisper: "God is good!"

The air is throbbing with the wings
Of birds, and bees, and fluttering things;
And all the world with song is rife,
With new-born hope and bounding life;
And Courage firmer sets his lance,
And Pleasure trips a lighter dance,

And Love and Joy make holiday
In all the smiling haunts of May;
And Faith grows strong, and Trust more true
As if themselves baptized with dew.

And thus would I, this glad, bright hour—
Where queenly Beauty builds her bower—
Share in the sweetness and the light
That fill the earth and banish night;
The infinite delight of song,
The power to triumph over wrong,
The grace, the patience to endure,
And faith in Heav'n, a purpose pure,
And all things fair, and good, and true,
Whose symbol is the stainless dew.

YOUR ENEMY.

Fear not, too much, an open enemy;
  He is consistent—always at his post;
But watchful be of him who holds the key
  Of your own heart, and flatters you the most.

MY SAILOR LAD.

My lover is a sailor lad,
  Upon the ocean blue,
On board a staunch and noble ship
  That bears a gallant crew.
And well I know, as days may go,
  Wherever he may sail,
His heart is constant as the sun,—
  His love will never fail.

At morn, the east is rosy red,
  And red, at eve, the west;
But neither morn, nor eve, can still
  The tumult of my breast,—
Nor yet the nights, whose starry lights,
  Like torches wax and wane,
While distant fares my sailor lad
  Upon the stormy main.

My prayers attend my sailor lad,
  Wherever he may be,
That never storm the ship may wreck
  To feed the hungry sea;
That kindly gales may fill her sails,
  And speed her homeward way;
And love shall crown my sailor lad—
  Forever and a day.

NOW.

I want no pledge of joys to be,—
  No false, uncertain vow;
That friend, alone, is kind to me
  Who proves his friendship now.

Life's changing year is brief, so brief,
  And I shall slumber long,
When autumn binds the yellow sheaf,
  And winter ends the song.

Then, sweetheart, come to-day and bring
  Love's flower in perfect bloom;
I shall not care what wreaths you fling
  To-morrow on my tomb.

BEYOND THE SUNSET HILLS.

I'd fain believe that when, at last,
　We quit life's joys and ills,
And when our toil-worn feet have passed
　Beyond the sunset hills,
That those who on this transient shore
　Walk with us, hand in hand,
Shall be our own forever more
　In a diviner land.
That all the rainbow round of flowers,
　That smile in beauty here,
Shall grace for us immortal bowers
　In that celestial sphere.
That all the tuneful birds we know,
　From dewy morn to even,
With sweeter songs shall overflow
　The purple hills of Heaven.

That earthly tasks that fail and fall,
    In weakness and disgrace,
Some day our hands shall finish all,
    With matchless skill and grace.
That in that palace of the skies,
    Whose walls with jasper gleam,
Shall forms of fairer mould arise
    Than fill the sculptor's dream;
The vision clear, by poets sought,
    Be ours, awaited long,
And every tender bud of thought
    Shall blossom into song.

FROM THE PERSIAN.

Malevolence, Envy and black Intrigue,
    Are up, and stirring, before the dawn;
And a rogue of a Lie will run a league
    While Truth is putting her sandals on.

SEMPER IDEM.

"Semper idem!" is here at the end
Of your little note, my gentle friend;
The sweetest phrase that the pen may trace
For a comrade-soul in the earthly race;
Fair and legible, over your name—
Words that signify—"ever the same."

Never, oh never that message true
Idly was written, my friend, by you!
Never, between us, a word unkind
Has marred, or broken the ties that bind;
And a strange, sweet joy, without a name,
Comes with your token—"ever the same."

But, will the light, as it used to do,
Sparkle and shine in your eyes of blue
When you think of me, as to and fro,
And wide apart in the world we go?

Will the dear, old friendship glow and flame
All the long journey—"ever the same?"

"Ever," my friend, is a long, long time;
It reaches far to a fairer clime—
A life beyond, and a brighter shore,
Where earth-born sorrows shall vex no more.
Will you know me there, and speak my name,
And gladden me always—"ever the same?"

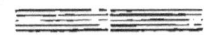

COUNTERPARTS.

The bee is lover of the flower,
And woos it every sunny hour;
The wave, enamoured of the star,
Reflects its beauty from afar;
The moonlight lances, pricking through
The forest leafage, find the dew;
And, somewhere, every loving heart
In God's world hath its counterpart.
And they shall come, in His good time,
To meet and beat in happy rhyme.

A BRIGHTER MORROW.

Dark cloud-flags wave above us,
  The squadrons of the rain
Bear down upon the forest,
  And sweep along the plain;
They break their shining lances
  Against our loved retreat,
And trample our sweet blossoms
  With swift, unsparing feet.
Yet, will our hearts be joyous,
  Nor grief, nor trouble borrow;
There cometh peace, the storm will cease—
  There'll be a brighter morrow!

So, when our lives are darkened,
  And clouds of ill hang o'er,
We'll never fear the sunshine
  Will fill the world no more.

"Let not your hearts be troubled!"
  Still kindly sayeth He
Whose mandate hushed the waters
  Of stormy Galilee.
He brings the balm of Gilead
  To heal the wounds of sorrow;
At his behest, there cometh rest—
  There'll be a brighter morrow!

Brave brother, art thou weary,
  And is the journey long?
Dear sister, dost thou falter,
  Has sorrow stilled thy song?
Rejoice! the sunset reddens,
  The clouds are rolling by,—
The glorious "bow of promise'
  Hangs in the eastern sky!
Thy heaven will be sweeter
  For days of earthly sorrow;
The storm will cease, there cometh peace—
  There'll be a brighter morrow!

THE ROSE OF THE PRAIRIE.

The dewdrops have vanished, the bee seeks the clover,
  To revel awhile in its sweetness and bloom,
But passes the blossoms our hands scatter over
  The little green roof of our lost darling's tomb.
She paled in the twilight, and died on the morrow,—
  She died in the morning of beauty and love;
The flowers drooped in sadness, the birds told their sorrow
  Aloud to each other in orchard and grove;
For every sweet thing loved the blithe, gentle Mary,
The pride of the household, the Rose of the Prairie!

She knew the sly nook where the blue-bird had hidden,
  Its bright, little eggs in a soft, downy nest,
And kept well the secret, lest strangers, unbidden,
  Should visit the place, and the treasures molest.
The faithful old dog by her side, in her rambles,
  Was never more faithful and constant, than she;
She shared with the lambkins their innocent gambols,
  And danced with the brook in its frolicsome glee,—
Their loving companion, the glad-hearted Mary,
The joy of the household, the Rose of the Prairie!

She joined the wood-thrush in the song he was singing,
  And warbled it sweetly the long summer day,
And stole from the rose, in the wilderness springing,
  One half of its glory and beauty away
To bloom on her cheek; and the violet peeping
  Up through the plumed grasses, beheld with surprise
Its purple-tinged azure so dreamily sleeping
  Far in the clear depths of her beautiful eyes.
So, every fair thing claimed a kinship with Mary,
The pride of the household, the Rose of the Prairie!

Alas! that the wild-bird, whose song is the essence
  Of music the sweetest, must carol alone!
Alas! that the blossoms which smiled in her presence
  Must wither and fade by the little, white stone
That marks the green grave of the sweetest of mortals
  That ever hath wandered on earth for a time,—
Whose feet have passed in through the great, pearly portals,
  Whose voice swells the anthem of glory sublime.
We murmur, in tears, "fare-thee-well, gentle Mary,
Lost joy of the household, the Rose of the Prairie!"

THE HUMMING-BIRD.

Hush! make no sound, nor move your finger-tips,—

A sprite, the Ariel of birds, is near!

The airy whisper of his wings I hear;

And now I see him, poising o'er the lips

Of my red columbine. His long bill dips

Into the waxen chalice where the clear,

Rich nectar lies. He trembles,—is it fear,

Or mad delight, that thrills him as he slips

From bloom to bloom, exacting honey-toll?

Sometimes unto my fancy, it appears

That this small vagrant, sensitive and coy,

Embodies a departed poet-soul,

To whom life brought,—but bitterness and tears;

And death,—a bird's delirium of joy!

THE DELLS.

I know a vale, a green retreat,
 Not long, nor deep, nor over-wide,
 Shut in by rocks on either side,
And starred with blossoms, honey-sweet.

My cloister in the woodland world,
 A dainty, Eden-bit it is
 Of nature (in parenthesis)
Where all her stormy flags are furled.

A great stone by the winding path
 Is worn, and hollowed, like a cup,—
 Where sparkling waters, welling up,
Might serve Diana for her bath.

In clustering globes the wild grapes swing
 From vines that lace and interlace
 The ranks of trees that crowd the place,—
And all the birds, my neighbors, sing.

This is the nook we call "The Dells;"
  And from "Diana's Bath" out flows
  A stream whose music as it goes
Is like the sound of silver bells.

Here in my hammock, swinging high,—
  Like some great spider in his web—
  Far from the strong, unceasing ebb
And flow of busy life, I lie,

And watch the dim leaf-shadows dance
  Upon the green, beside the brook;
  Or read from some well-treasured book
Some pleasing tale of old romance,

Or, con my favorite poet's words
  And drink their soul of music rare
  Until my soul, absolved from care,
Soars—singing with the singing birds.

Dear Mother-Nature! thou art kind,
  And in thy temples, sweet and calm,
  Are, for the weary body, balm,—
And balsam for the troubled mind!

Thou bringest joy to him who dwells

   With thee, and worships at thy shrine,—

   Who helps, not mars, thy fair design,

And reads thy secrets in "The Dells."

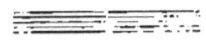

THE ORIOLE.

In robe of orange, and of black,

   With mellow music in his throat,

Our fairest summer bird is back

   From southern woods and fields remote.

Beneath the shading, glossy leaves

   The sunset gold upon his breast—

The restless, little toiler weaves

   His hanging wonder of a nest!

And, as I watch him, flashing there,

   My fancy deems the oriole

A wand'ring blossom of the air,

   Endowed with wings, and voice, and soul!

48

LEONORE.

Leonore, the snow is falling,
　Fairy-like, and spotless white!
And my soul to you is calling
　Far across the starless night!
Lean your golden head to hear me,
　As you heard me long ago;
And as noiselessly draw near me
　As the feather-footed snow!

Bring to me the starry splendor
　Of the love-light in your eyes;
Never light more sweet and tender
　Lit a soul to Paradise.
Past the wide and deep abysses
　Of ''the night's Plutonian shore,''
Bring to me the honey-kisses
　Of your red lips, Leonore!

Vain my cry!   A phantom, only,
　　Mocks my spirit's wild unrest;
Empty is my heart, and lonely
　　As a long deserted nest!
Neither prayer, nor vigil-keeping,
　　Lifts the burden of my woe,
Leonore, for you are sleeping,
　　Dreamless now, beneath the snow!

IN REVERY.

In revery, with moveless lips,
　　My lady sits, for hours and hours,
The while, in silver sandals, trips
　　The laughing rain among her flowers.

Her life a sorrow holds—and yet,
　　The sweet and sympathetic rain
May serve to soften her regret,
　　And lull and lighten all the pain.

BEN MURAD.

Ben Murad, caliph,—great his fame—
Gave audience to all who came,
That he might learn what wrongs, what grief
His people bore, and give relief.

Two men before the dais stood;
A woman, veiled, Zuleika—good.
"Attend! whose trouble is the worst,"
The caliph said, "shall speak the first!"

"My husband has deserted me!"
Bemoaned the woman piteously.
"Alzerah is a graceless dog,"
The caliph said, "the rogue we'll flog!"

"Robbed of my gems—no loss beside
So great as mine!" Noureddin cried.
"Who plies such bold, such shameless trade,"
The caliph said, "we'll bastinade!"

"My grief is cruelest of all;
Selim is stolen from his stall!"
Mustapha wailed. The caliph said,
"Who is the thief—shall lose his head!"

"Zuleika! small your cause to weep;
Noureddin! all your gems are cheap;
But loss of steed is woe accurst,—
Mustapha should have spoken first!"

EVE AT MT. TACOMA.

In the pine-green zone, that curves and sweeps
  To measure the mountain's perimeter,
The vireos's song, outwearied, sleeps,
And down the blue west the new moon creeps,
  And cuts a white cloud with its scimeter!

ROBERT BURNS.

O, Scotland, land of glory,
　Of story and of song!
What thoughts thy name awakens,
　What golden memories throng
Upon us of thy grandeur,
　Thy greatness and thy pride;
Thy rugged rocks and mountains,
　Thy men in battle tried;
Heroic Bruce and Wallace!
　To them the vision turns,
But lingers last and longest
　On glorious Robert Burns!

A lowly Ayrshire peasant,
　Whose soul was all in tune;
Whose song was bright and flowing
　As waves of "Bonny Doon;"
In haunts of mirth and pleasure,

Where lads and lassies meet,
With him, we hear the bag-pipes;
We list the tripping feet,
In rhythmic measure dancing,
  And plaided bosoms swell;
Here blows the mountain daisy,
  There blooms the heather-bell!

The "Cotter's Hymn" is floating
  Upon the winter air;
We urge in solemn cadence
  The "priest-like father's" prayer;
We ken the "frost untimely;"
  We see the trickling tear
That falls for "Highland Mary,"
  And "Bonnie Jean" is here.
At Bannockburn we're with him
  In thickest of the fight;
At "Auld Kirk Alloway" again,
  At "witching hour" of night;
While gently still the waters
  Of fair, "sweet Afton" flow;
And all the world remembers
  "John Anderson, my Jo!"

The snows of scores of winters
  About his tomb have whirled,
Yet still the bard goes singing
  His way around the world.
And precious to his spirit,
  As e'er it earthward turns,
Must be the love that hallows
  The deathless name of Burns.
The wide world crowns thy poet—
  To him all hearts belong,
O, Scotland, land of glory,
  Of story and of song.

THE SWEETEST SONG.

That song is sweetest, bravest, best,
  Which plucks the thistle-barb of care
From a despondent brother's breast,
  And plants a sprig of heart's-ease there.

THE BLUE-BIRD.

I saw a pretty blue-bird, yesterday,
Rocking itself upon a budding spray—
The while it fluted forth a tender song
'That brought a promise of sunshiny days.

It is the loveliest little bird that comes
In early spring-time to our northern homes.
We note its presence, bid it welcome here,
Before the crocus its green calyx parts
To lead the smiling sisterhood of flowers
In fair procession through the summer land.
The sweet-voiced warbler wears a coat that mocks
The hue of violet, or trumpet-flower,
Or the blue larkspur.

                    Oftentimes a bar
Of music, or the drowsy hum of bees
In an old orchard, or the faintest scent
Of a familiar blossom, leads us back

Along the track of years, to sights and sounds
Of long ago. So, ever, when I hear
The blue-bird caroling its perfect song—
Whose harshest note breathes only love and peace—
And when I mark its brilliant uniform,—
This midget bird, so small that it might be
Imprisoned in a lady's lily hand—
I am reminded of the battle years
When men, full-armed, and wearing suits of blue,
Marched to the music of the fife and drum
In strong battalions in a southern land.
And all the pomp and blazonry of war,—
Guidons and banners tossing in the breeze,
Sabers and muskets glinting in the sun,
Carriage and caisson rumbling o'er the stones,
The midnight vigil of the lone vidette,
The shock and roar of battle, and the shouts
Of the victorious army when the fight
Was done; the aftermath of sorrows deep,—
The cries and moans of wounded, dying men,
The hurried burial of the dead at night,
The broken lives in many homes, the hearths
Made desolate,—all these come back to me,
As I beheld and knew them, once; and then,

In sad reflection to myself I sigh:
What weak, inglorious fools we mortals are
That war must be, or any need of war.

And yet, the better day is coming when
The teachings of the lowly Nazarene
Shall be the rule of nations,—as of men;
The sword and bayonet shall be preserved,
By the fair children of a nobler race,
As relics only, of a barbarous past
When men were crazed, and shed each others' blood.
All souls shall be in touch and harmony
With Nature, and her higher, holier laws;
And all the world, from farthest sea to sea,
Shall know a sweet, idyllic peace and rest,
Unmarred by strife, or any harsher sounds
Than her harmonious voices—ocean waves,
Breaking in rhythmic beat upon the shore;
The murmurous solo of the valley brook,—
The wind's wild monody amid the pines,—
The thrush's whistle, and the bluebird's song.

OCTOBER'S AMBER DAYS.

Now come October's amber days
  In loveliness untold,
And sprinkle all the woodland ways
  As with a dust of gold.

And leaves are red as ruby wine,
  Or stained with purple dyes;
Yet, heavily this heart of mine
  Within my bosom lies.

It was a fair October day
  That brimmed my cup with grief,
When my beloved passed away,
  As falls the autumn leaf.

A sudden tremor of the lips,
  Foretold the soul's release,
And then, the shade of death's eclipse,
  And God's eternal peace!

Dear Soul! I wonder if she knows
　My loneliness to-night?—
How sorrow bides, and gladness goes,
　And every pure delight?

Her love,—what words can measure it?
　It was a heavenly spark,—
The one sweet star whose brightness lit
　My pathway in the dark.

Her dear companionship I miss,—
　I miss her cheering words;
Her heart was tender as her kiss,
　Yet sunny as a bird's.

No plaint of helpless youth or age
　Appealed to her in vain,
Or found her tardy to assuage
　The lightest grief or pain.

So when the queen October gives
　The world her crimson sign,
Back in the past my spirit lives,—
　Its sadness all is mine.

Yet one assuring thought will come
To ease the bitter dole,—
That she who shared, and blessed my home,
Is now an angel-soul.

❦❦❦❦●❦❦❦❦

MY SAINT.

'Twas Christmas-tide. I count the woman saint.
Serene and beautiful, and high of soul,
I almost thought to see the aureole
About her head—as Christ the masters paint.
No crucifix, nor rosary, she bore—
Albeit, one by one she told as beads,
Such joy-bestowing and unselfish deeds
As the All-Father blesses evermore.

The sweet, perpetual sunlight of her smile
A chrism was, for heavy hearts, and bruised—
Her lightest touch did weary pain beguile;
She hushed the widow's and the orphan's plaint,
And tears of thankfulness all eyes suffused.
None knew her name, or place. She is my saint.

OUR DAILY BREAD.

"Give us this day our daily bread!"
Each morn, in prayer, Jim Williams said.

A stalwart man, with brawny arm,
And owner of a splendid farm,
He toiled but little in the field,
And scant the hoard, and small the yield;
The pirate weeds destroyed his corn,
Untrimmed remained his hedge of thorn;
His gates were old, his fences down—
Much time he spent in Morristown;
Paid much for missions, chapels, pews,
The while his children wanted shoes.

His nearest neighbor, William Lee,
Was not renowned for piety;
Yet William, up before the sun,
Fought long and hard—life's battle won.

And once, I know, I heard him say:
"If I am ever called to pray
Unto the Lord to give to me
My 'daily bread' I'll try to be
A little more in tune with Him
Than is, I think, my neighbor Jim.
I'll plow the field and sow the seed
That He may bid the harvest speed;
And He will know I ask for bread,
Though not a word of prayer be said!"

In this discourse, it seems to me,
That Farmer Lee's philosophy
Is wholesome, wise, and sound of grain—
The doctrine good, the moral plain,
To wit: That he who will not work,—
Who is as lazy as a Turk,
Has little right to ask the Lord
To bless him with the same reward
That follows effort, brave and true,—
That comes to labor as its due;
Has little right to bow the head,
And pray: "Give us our daily bread!"

AMONG THE ROSES.

Each hour discloses
Some new delight that summer yields—
To fill her gardens, and her fields;
Some blither song-bird's minstrelsy,
Some sweeter sweets to lure the bee—

Amid her posies;
Some fairer charm, of form or hue,
Some brighter chalice brimmed with dew,
Some richer wealth of rare perfume,
Some deeper blush, some lovelier bloom—

Among the roses.

So life discloses—
Howe'er the pathway curve or turn—
New hopes that rise, new stars that burn
In changing splendor night or day;
New joys that drive old griefs away—

Ere Death disposes;

New lessons learned, new trophies won,

New windows open to the sun,

New treasures found, with little quest,

New grottoes reached, where Toil may rest —

Among the roses.

DEMENTIA.

The man is mad!   A lone and shattered bark,

Sans ballast, rudder, compass, helplessly

He drifts upon the wide, tempestuous sea;

Nor ray of moon, nor star, nor beacon spark,

In heaven, or on the shore, illumes the dark,

And shows the place where deadly breakers be,

That smite the rocks, and roar upon the lee

And fling white corpses of drowned sailors stark

Upon the beach.

"Our Father," pity him!

Dispel the mists that cloud the errant brain.

Set Thou the ship in order,—spar and mast,

Pennon, and sail; and guide her, stout and trim,

With clear-eyed Reason at the helm again,

Into the harbor of Thy rest at last!

THE DAISY IN THE SOUTH.

[A Southern man, who visited Washington recently, told a reporter of THE POST that the daisy was never known in the South until after the war. Now it is abundant in every locality visited by the Union Army, and the line of Sherman's march can be followed by keeping where the daisy grows. The seed seems to have been transported in the hay that was brought along to feed the horses. That is the only explanation that has ever been given of it.]

There's a story told in Georgia—
  'Tis in everybody's mouth—
That 'twas old "Tecumseh" Sherman
  Brought the daisy to the South.

Ne'er the little blossom-stranger
  In that land was known to be
Till he marched his bluecoat columns
  From Atlanta to the sea.

Everywhere, in field and valley,
  And the murm'ring pines among,
Where a gallant Union soldier
  Pressed his foot, a daisy sprung;

And its coming seemed to many
　Like a promise from on high,
Given them in benediction,
　When "Old Glory" floated by.

Where the troopers fed their horses
　Where the "bummers" bivouacked,
Now with each recurring summer,
　All that highway may be tracked
By the glory of the presence—
　As the stars the sky illume—
Of a million Northern daisies
　In the beauty of their bloom.

Thus the kindly hand of Nature
　Hides the scars that war has made;
Vines entwine the shattered musket,
　Blossoms wreathe the broken blade
Timid, tiny birds have nested
　Safely in the cannon's mouth
Ever since the year that Sherman
　Brought the daisy to the South.

JOHN ERICSSON.

Died, March 8th, 1889.

He rests in sweet, untroubled sleep—
  The brave old man! His toil is done;
And Fame his name will proudly keep
  While coming years their cycles run.

His was the genius, and the skill,
  The hand that wrought, the brain that planned
To save the state from direst ill
  When War and Havoc ruled the land.

"I'll build," said he, "a wonder-boat,
  An Amazon to sail the seas,
And cope with any craft afloat
  That braves the battle and the breeze."

'Twas done,—the merest speck she seemed,
  To eyes that watched her from afar,
As, all equipped, and manned, she steamed
  Across the harbor's outer bar.

Forth into Hampton Roads there sailed,
　One day, the dreaded Merrimack—
The rebel ram, with iron mailed—
　A scaly monster, huge and black.

Straight down the broadening bay she bore,
　Destroying every ship she met—
To where, upon the ocean-floor,
　The Monitor, a sea vidette.

Paced to and fro across her path;
　'Twas man-of-war against a toy;
'Twas as Goliath, him of Gath,
　And Israel's slender shepherd-boy.

The pigmy parried well the stroke
　Whose weight was many a thousand tons,
And in her iron turret woke
　From sleep her thunder-throated guns.

The heavy missiles fell like hail;
　They rent and pierced the monster's hide,
Crushed beam and rib, broke plate and scale,
　And sent her helpless down the tide.

A famous battle, nobly won!

   Honor the gallant men who fought;

But honor most John Ericsson,

   Who brought the foeman's power to naught!

And ever green his memory keep,

   As countless years their cycles run,

The while he sleeps in dreamless sleep,

   The brave old man whose work is none.

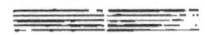

DANDELIONS.

   Bright coinage of the generous sun,

   Down-flung, and scattered, one by one—

   They star with gold the green plateau,

   And light the landscape with their glow!

THE POET. •

Composite is the poet's character,
And who may be its true interpreter,
Or measure what his mission comprehends—
Where it begins, or where his influence ends?
For he hath many offices—the least
A noble one—as teacher, prophet, priest,
Painter and sculptor, guide and architect—
To plan, to build, to counsel and direct—
And almoner of Heav'n's divinest gifts;
His song an angel's pinion that uplifts
The souls of men to every lofty height,
High as the stars that sparkle in the night.

The service he hath rendered antedates
That of the priests, at Israel's temple-gates;
And he hath lain rare gifts, and homage due,
On every altar to the Good and True;

And knelt, a worshipper, at every shrine
Of Virtue, Beauty, and all things divine.
And he the Delphic oracles hath heard,—
The sage's utterance, and the prophet's word,
And, by the magic of his potent pen,
Brought all their helpful messages to men.

Nay more: Where wrong meets Right with rapier-thrust
Where gaunt-faced Famine clamors for a crust,
Where bright-eyed Joy is changed to crouching Fear,
And Grief demands the tribute of a tear;
Where brooding Sorrow sits beside the tomb,
And Hope expires amid the gath'ring gloom,—
His kindness falls, his benefactions throng
With all the tender ministry of song,—
A healing balm, the anodyne of pain,
Free as the air, and gentle as the rain.

A painter, too, he paints the myriad forms
Of changeful Nature, in her calms and storms;
The mountain daisy in its cloister-nook,—
The yellow cowslip by the meadow brook,
The sev'n-fold colors of the rainbow fair,
The rich cloud-argosies that sail the air,
The wide expanse of the unfathomed sky,—
An azure sea where argent islands lie—

The feath'ry crystals of the arctic snows,
"White as the Cyprian foam whence Venus rose;"
The borealis' flaming aureole,
Lighting the heavens above the distant pole;
And woods and waters, seas and smiling lands,
Hills, mountains, vales, Sahara's arid sands;
Tracing them all in vivid arabesque
On the white tablet, lying on his desk.

He knows the privacies of birds and bees,
And holds a comradeship with all the trees.
Beneath their boughs, where darkling shadows fall,
Dryads, and hamadryads, wait his call;
And elves, and fairies, that in moonlight dance,
Come when he beckons—recognize his glance;
Naiads, and nereids, comb their yellow locks,
And smile a welcome from their wave-girt rocks.

He knows the genii that set in strife
The warring elements that threaten life,
When leaps the lightning from its cloudy lair
To shake the tresses of its fiery hair;
When hoarse-voiced thunder bellows in the rain,
Like angry bulls, in combat on the plain;

Simoon, sirocco, hurricane and gale,
Wherein the women shriek, the men turn pale.
And the soft zephyr, that so gently blows
It scarcely moves the petals of the rose,
Their subtle scent and sweetness to disperse;
All these he paints, or photographs, in verse.

The only pigments, ready to his hand,
Are words, dead words—the language of the land;
His finger touches them, and they become
Alive and luminous—no longer dumb.
With these he pictures every mortal man,
The living and the dead, since time began,
In fairer lines, and deeper, richer glow
Than all the saints of Michael Angelo.

His art portrays the very souls of men,
And things intangible, beyond our ken,
His finer, deeper spiritual sense
Discerning all the Past, the Now and Hence,—
Not only that which is, but that which seems—
Dreams, and the shadowy scenery of dreams.

And, as the sculptor wakes from marble sleep
A heavenly goddess evermore to keep
In Art's grand Pantheon a chosen place,

He moulds and shapes, with matchless skill and grace,
From Truth's Carrara-block the lovely form
Of saint, or seraphim—and makes it warm,
Instinct with throbbing life, until we see
And feel it near, a breathing entity—
All this with more of power creative shown
"Than Phidias dreamed of when he wrought the stone."

In his ideal world he plans and builds
A thousand stately towers and temples,—gilds
Their lofty domes, and minarets, and spires,
With all the ruddy glow of sunset fires;
Rears grander arches, lovelier arcades,
Transepts, and pediments, and colonnades,
Than boasts that ancient pile, of wondrous dome—
Saint Peter's church, the heart and pride of Rome.

But most, as guide and teacher of the race,
He holds a lofty and an honored place;
Takes tottering Age and Childhood by the hand,
And leads them through a flower-besprinkled land;
Sets lamps of joy, of memory, and of hope,
To light the falling and the rising slope;
Brings grace to manhood never known before,
And adds a tithe to Learning's gathered store;

Knits closer still the ties of brotherhood.

'Twixt man and man; conserves the highest good;

Teaches the worth of temperance and ruth,

And the eternal unity of Truth;

That every soul, though sin-obscured and dim,

Is kin to God, and somewhere touches Him.

His pen, betimes, is like a falchion strong

To smite, and break the scales of armoured Wrong,

And wrest from Fraud its undeserving crown;

A whip to scourge the tiger-passions down,

A lightning dart, a fiery javelin

To slay the wolves of Treachery and Sin,

Transfix the vampire, Hate, that comes and goes,

And prick the airy bubbles Folly blows.

But greatest he when he interprets best

The feelings born in every human breast;

All warm, glad thoughts, and fair and undefiled—

The tie that binds the mother to her child,

And Friendship's sweets, and all the loves we know

In life's swift round, and every joy and woe.

This power to touch the universal chord

Confirms his high commission from the Lord.

THE GREEN AND GOLD.

The breeze across the hills of morn
  Is fair, and fresh, and sweet;
Green are the fields of waving corn,
  And gold the fields of wheat.

These leagues of lustrous green enfold
  A hope, whereon we build;
And these proclaim—these leagues of gold—
  A prophecy fulfilled.

They hint, they tell, that all is well
  In all the splendid land;
They promise bounty, full and free,
  As from a kingly hand.

Around the burnished, yellow squares
  The busy reapers ply;
With whirr and hum, they go and come,
  They wheel, and hurry by.

From early morn to set of sun
   They speed, and gather in;
They seize, and hold, the harvest gold,
   To heap the harvest bin.

And many a deep and throbbing joy,
   And many a pleasure sweet,
Were never born but for the corn,
   And for the golden wheat.

THE RED BIRD.

When the summer sky is a tent of blue,
   And rosy June is the regnant queen,
A crimson shuttle, he flashes through
   The leafy warp of the forest green.

And the thread of a sweet song follows him,
   In mazy tangles of shade and sun,
And stretches away in the distance dim—
   And the bonny bird, and the song—are one!

ASPIRATION.

In every free and conscious human soul
  There lives a spark of the Promethean fire,—
  Infinite longings, hopes that aye aspire
To reach a higher life, a fairer goal,
Whence carking care, and all the bitter dole
  Of earth-born sorrows,—clouds, and darkness dire
  That hide the stars, and foil the soul's desire—
Have passed away, as from the green hills roll
The morning mists. Before us, tall and white,
  The silent peaks of grand sierras rise,
    Bathed in the glory of the noonday sun;
Mount after mount we climb, to touch the height
  Of life's supreme endeavor. So, the skies
    Are gained, and Heaven's jewel-splendors won.

MEMORIAL DAY.

Hushed, now, is the warlike drum,
  And the bugle sounds no more;
And the lips of the cannon are dumb
  In the land—from shore to shore.

Like a faded glory-wreath
  The battle-flag hangs on the wall,—
And the saber sleeps in its sheath
  In silent chamber and hall.

And the little children go
  To hold their innocent sports
In the bastions, leveled low,
  Of the old dismantled forts.

Peace, peace, with her snowy wings,
  Broods over valley and height;
And war, and the sorrow it brings,
  Have gone—like a dream of the night.

A feverish dream to the wife,
Or the tearful mother, who sent
The joy and the pride of her life
With the new formed regiment.

'Tis not forgotten by those
Who shared in the rough campaign,
And stood where the iron blows
Of the battle fell like rain.

For many came back no more
Out of the sulphurous smoke,—
Out of the clamor and roar,
When the storm of the conflict broke.

Wasted by wounds and disease,
Fevers and pests in the swamps,
Perished those heroes—and these,
Died in the prison-camps.

Brave as the olden knights,
Grandly they followed the flag,
Scaling the perilous heights
Of Victory's eyrie-crag.

Perchance, from their spectral camps.
　In the mystic fields above,
Where the stars are their censer lamps,
　Even now, they note our love,

And whisper, thus, spirit-wise,
　To each other, again and again:
"They remember our sacrifice—
　Lo! we have not died in vain!"

Then honor the sleeping braves,
　Forever, and ever and aye,
And rainbow the green of their graves
　With the beautiful flowers of May.

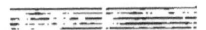

GOLDEN ROD.

It burns and broadens, and flashes and smiles,
And stretches away for a thousand miles.
'Tis the shining path the Infinite trod
To measure the earth with His golden rod!

AUF WIEDERSEHEN.

I like, full well, that friendly German phrase,
   "Auf Wiedersehen!" It hath a cheerier tone,
   I deem, than any farewell greeting known
To English speech, and heard, we go our ways,
Not wholly comfortless, in all the days
   To come, though we may wander long and lone,
   In paths apart. It holds a bud unblown
Of sweetest hope, whose promise cheers, and stays
The soul. Not so our homely, trite "Good-Bye;"
   There's sadness in it,—and the word "Farewell"
   Hath syllables that sob like winter rain.
Both seem a separation to imply
   That may, perhaps, be final,—who can tell?
   So, when we part, I'll say "Auf Wiedersehen!"

CHRISTINE.

I met her in the spring-time,
   When all the woods were green—
The snow of apple-blossoms
   Was drifting o'er the scene—
A maiden, tall and stately,
     A very woodland queen,—
     My love, my fair Christine!

Her beauty flashed upon me
   In many a wildering ray,
In dreams, a glorious vision
   That faded not by day,
It filled me, and it thrilled me,
     And stole my heart away—
     Ah well, ah well-a-day!

I meet her in the meadow,
   I greet her on the hill;
Her cheeks' unrivaled roses
   For me are blooming still,

And oh! her voice is sweeter
　　Than silver-singing rill,
　　Or any song-bird's trill!

And when the frosts of autumn
　　Transform the woodlands green
To brown, and gold, and crimson,
　　I'll wed with her I ween,
And bide beside her ever,
　　For she's my chosen queen,—
　　My peerless love, Christine!

☙☙☙☙●❧❧❧❧

AT THE SEASIDE.

All day the mist-buckets, let down by the sun,
　　Have carried the moisture from ocean to cloud;
And now the wee rain-drops, my dear, have begun
　　To fall from the sky—on the humble and proud.

A benison truly—the soft, salty spray
　　Has brightened the roses for you, and for me;
And we, and the blossoms, are ready to say:
　　How kind, after all, is the restless, old sea!

TO ESTELLE.

What gift of mine can make amends
For the sweet joy your friendship lends
To me, O gentlest of my friends?

How merrily, that morn in May,
The birds sang songs that seemed to say:
"O happy day! O happy day!"

Before me, tall and fair, you stood,—-
A graceful Phyllis of the wood,
A queenly queen of womanhood.

The tender azure of the sky,
Serene and cloudless, scarce could vie
In calmness with your calm blue eye.

So cordially your greeting came,—
So pleasantly you spoke my name,
My cheek was lit with sudden flame.

'A maiden free from every guile!"
I murmured to myself the while
I drank the sunshine of your smile.

And since that day—as'days go by—
The starry worlds that gem the sky,
The brooklet's silver lullaby,

The flowers that bloom in solitude,
In the green cloisters of the wood,
And all things beautiful and good,

Remind me of the fair and young,
Sweet girl for whom my harp is strung,—
For whom this little song is sung;

The peerless maid who long, and well,
Has bound me with her subtle spell,—
My rare, true friend, my own Estelle!

THE WHEAT HARVEST.

Miles and miles, before the eye,
Near and far, the wheat fields lie
Ripening, goldening, one by one,
Shimmering, glimmering in the sun,
As the south wind through them all
Makes the yellow billows fall—
Rise and fall, in cadence sweet—
Wavering, quavering through the wheat.

Let me tell you, if you please,
What in this a dreamer sees;
What the brightness and the gold
Of the fields to him unfold;
What the minstrel south wind sings,
In its mystic whisperings,
As his listening ear they greet
In the waving of the wheat.

Now, behold! an army comes!
Not with trumpets, nor with drums;
Not with chariot, spear and shield,
As of old, they seek the field;
But the chariots they drive
Seem like creatures, all alive.
How they clatter, clank and clink—
Weary not, and almost think.

'Tis a wonderful machine!
With its sickle bright and keen,
With its pulleys, belts and reels
Rods and cogs, and many wheels;
With its strong, far-reaching arms,
Swinging on a thousand farms,
Gathering in the golden grain
Of the harvest, on the plain—
Leaving in its wake the sheaves
Thick as Vallambrosa's leaves.

Fair beneath the sunny skies
Towering pyramids arise—
Broad, and round, and all complete—
Of the heavy-headed wheat.
Then the thresher plies his trade,

In his dusty ambuscade,
And a wide capacious spout
Lets the amber riches out.
Ingots, golden eagles, gleam
In that swiftly flowing stream—
Silver dollars, large and round,
For the tillers of the ground.

All of these, and more than these,
Proudly, now, the master sees;
For his toil a full reward
In the bounty of the Lord;
Respite from a hundred woes,
That hath robbed him of repose,
With their worry and their fret;
Freedom from the bonds of debt—
From the milldew, deep and green,
Of the mortgage and the lien.

For himself, at length, he sees
Greater leisure, more of ease;
For the patient, loving wife,
Richer comforts, fuller life;
Books and music for the girls,
(Sweet and fair as clustered pearls;)

For the sturdy, helpful boys,
Higher pleasures, nobler joys;
Peace and Plenty, hand in hand,--
All his world a Canaan land.

These the pleasant sights that come
To the dreamer in his home,
Gazing on a summer day,
"O'er the hills, and far away;"
These the songs the winds repeat,
Mystic, musical and sweet,
In the waving of the wheat!

KEEP SUNSHINE IN THE HEART.

Keep sunshine in the heart, my friend,
  Whatever may betide;
Though clouds hang dark above thy path,
  And faith be sorely tried.
Though friends have cold and distant grown,
  Nor longer lend their aid,
Smile on, smile on, and falter not—
  In sunshine, or in shade.

For grief will be of no avail,—
  Its tears will weaken thee;
But joy will make thee strong, and set
  The prisoned spirit free.
The happy birds will sing again,
  The winter will not stay,
And fair in wood and field will spring
  The blossoms of the May.

Thy wand'ring friends will soon return,
  As brothers, to thy side,
And lend thee still a hand to stem
  Misfortune's darkling tide.

Then let thy poor repinings cease,
　Thy gloomy fears depart;
Keep sunshine in the heart, my friend,—
　Keep sunshine in the heart!

MOONRISE.

I saw the round moon rising from the sea,
　One summer evening from a lonely isle
　Hard by the northern coast.　A ruined pile,
Seat of some ancient lord of Brittany,
Revealed its lines in ghostly tracery,
　As o'er the placid waves for many a mile
　The mellow moonlight, "like a silver Nile,"
Came floating, flowing, pulsing down to me.

I stood in mute bewilderment, entranced;
　That throbbing mystery, the ocean, seemed
With all its might and mystery enhanced,
　In the white radiance over all that streamed;
And the enchantment, as the night advanced,
　Was deeper, sweeter than my soul had dreamed!

THE SWEETEST ROSE.

"The sweetest rose, of fairest hue,"
The lady said, "I'll give to you,
  Here at the gate, the while we wait,
  This summer night!" The hour was late,
And arrow-swift the moments flew.

The star-lights twinkled in the blue—
The leaves were jeweled with the dew.
  "And you," she said, "may designate
  .   The sweetest rose!"

The suitor well his vantage knew,
Aside his fears and tremblings threw,
  And hurried headlong to his fate.
  "I choose the rose beside the gate;
It is," he said, "as Truth is true—
    The sweetest rose!"

A PICTURE.

So long as honest men neglect to vote;

So long as good men leave the cares of state

To weak, incompetent, or careless hands,

Or place them in the grip of scheming knaves,

Our safety is imperilled.   Every man

On Freedom's ramparts must a warder be,

To warn of danger when the foe appears;

To meet the onset when the foe assaults.

Else—vain our hopes, and else the .temple grand,

Of all our rights, and birth-right liberties,

Ere long will fall, and crumble in the dust,

A ruin, more abject and dire than Rome

Or Carthage was.

          The power that rules must be

The will of all; the strength, in aggregate,

The courage, conscience, sense of justice true,

And wisdom of the people—so expressed
That every voice is heard. If this be not,
Base men, and demagogues, will ply their trade,
Defraud and plunder, misdirect affairs.
The greed and avarice of the lordly few
Will trample on the many, rob the poor,
And cheat the laborer of his rightful wage.

Then Discontent will mutter, loud and long,
And all the hurtful, hateful, hellish "isms,"
By errant cranks, and lunatics, begot,
Will spread and flourish till at length a mine
Of dynamite is placed beneath the stones
Whereon our social fabric rests. And when
Some mountain blunder, baser than a crime,
Outrages public sense of decency,
And right, and justice—lo! the mine is sprung!
Nor all the bayonets the smiths have forged,
From Washington to Cleveland, can restore
The temple's broken columns, once so fair.

How do you like the picture? Is it true,
Or false, or partly both? If true, you hold
In your own hands the remedy. Do right!

Mete justice, equal and exact, to all;
Bear equal burdens with your fellow men;
Discharge your every duty faithfully
Unto your God, your country, and yourselves;
When your white ballots flutter down like leaves
In autumn, see that wisdom guides their fall;
Choose no unworthy man to serve the state;
Withhold no help from him who has been true
And faithful to the common weal. This done—
Year after year, from Oregon to Maine,
From Minnesota to the Southern gulf,
By every freeman worthy of the name,
The great and proud Republic of the West
Will live, and triumph, for a thousand years!

DEACON PETTIBONE.

Good Deacon Silas Pettibone—
    For so the record runs—
Though rather old and feeble grown,
    Was fond of making puns.
He saw the comic side of life,
    And often when he spoke—
To friend or stranger, child or wife,—
    Would have "his little joke."

His neighbor King, and he it seems,
    Had mutual dislike,
And almost went to such extremes
    As bring about a "strike."
A fractious filly chanced to fling
    Old King. Said Pettibone:
"Although I do not love the King,
    I will approach the thrown!"

He strolled one eve beside the sea,
    Along a shady beach,

And heard a couple piteously
  Complaining, each to each.
Young Newleigh Wedde was standing near
  Beside his pouting bride.
"Alas!" said Pettibone, "I hear
  The moaning of the tied!"

When Pettibone was sick in bed,
  In walked his nephew, Lee;
"I came to see," the rascal said,
  "If you will lend a V."
The uncle said, "your wondrous cheek
  Much folly may atone;
And yet, with purse and person weak,
  I cannot stand a loan!"

The jolly Deacon died, at last,
  Whose jokes made many laugh;
But, just before his spirit passed,
  He wrote this epitaph:
"Here lie, beneath this truthful stone,—
  Some larger bones among—
The petty bones of Pettibone,
  Whose heart was always young!"

A SUMMER NIGHT.

The warm, long day is ended,
  The cooler night prevails;
In blue seas, calm and splendid,
The new moon, star-attended,
  A white gondola, sails.

The mad-cap winds are quiet,
  They set no leaf astir,
As if, by nature's fiat,
Were stilled their playful riot,
  Lest it discomfort her.

The elfin, minstrel cricket,
  With listless, drooping wings,
Sits by the little wicket,
That guards his grassy thicket—
  And drowsily he sings.

The thrush is in her bower,
  The sparrow in her nest,
And every folded flower
Has yielded to the power
  That lulls the world to rest.

I read your message tender,
  And own your influence, too,—
And all my soul surrender,
Oh night, of peace and splendor—
  Of starlight and of dew!

SHIP FROM FORTUNE'S ISLE.

My neighbor, home returned from sea,
    Where he has voyaged long,
Sings oft, to please the girls and boys,
    A pleasant, sailor song.
I've heard it half a score of times,
    And so have you, no doubt;
"The ship that sailed from Fortune's Isle"
    Is what 'tis all about.

According to the song, my lad,
    She is a vessel fine
As ever spread, or reefed a sail,
    Or ever crossed "the Line,"
Complete and neat and trim aloft,
    And snug and strong below—
"The ship that sailed from Fortune's Isle,"
    So long, so long ago.

She carries worlds of costly goods,
    And gems, and bags of gold

And silver,—half of which the Bank
  Of England would not hold.
And much of all this wealth, 'tis said.
  Will come to you and me
In that good "ship from Fortune's Isle,"
  Across the Carib sea.

She bears some bales of lovers' dreams,
  Bound up in ribbons blue,
And when she reaches port at last,
  The dreams will all come true.
And many a high, heroic soul
  Will fame and glory win
The day "the ship from Fortune's Isle"
  Comes proudly sailing in.

Beyond the harbor's outer bar,
  Against the deep, blue sky,
God grant we soon shall sight her sail,
  And see her pennon fly,
And welcome home with all the stores
  She bears for you and me,
The gallant "ship from Fortune's Isle"
  That sailed the Carib sea!

THE HEART WILL REMEMBER.

When life burns to ashes that hold but an ember,—
A fast-fading spark of their olden-time glow—
The head may forget, but the heart will remember
The deeper delights of the days long ago.
A mother's devotion, unfailing, unbounded,
Her loving caresses, her smiles and her tears;
A sister's affection no plummet hath sounded,
No tempest hath ruffled in all the long years.

Another—a vision of beauty and splendor
That Time and his shadows can never eclipse—
Comes back in the gloaming, with eyes soft and tender,
And thrills you again with the touch of her lips.
The world is enchanted, a wonderful palace,
Dream-built and celestial, inviting repose;
You drink the rich draught of a nectar-brimmed chalice,
And life is as fragrant and sweet as the rose.

It may be that still in your memory lingers
　A child's artless prattle, with love in its tone,
The sweet pressure felt of a baby's soft fingers—
　White, clinging and dimpled—entwined with your own
Nor darkness, nor slumber, effaces the token
　That Sorrow, unbidden, once came as your guest;
That voice has been hushed into silence unbroken,—
　Those hands now are folded in infinite rest.

Your steps may be slow, and your locks may be hoary,—
　Approaching the end of your pilgrimage here;
And yet, the recital of one little story,
　Like rain in the desert, will freshen and cheer.
No matter what treasures, from May to December,—
　What favors of fortune have come at your call—
The head may forget, but the heart will remember
　That Love was the jewel outshining them all!

THE BELLS OF BROOKLINE.

[The news of Lee's surrender at Appomattox first came to Brookline, Mass., through a private dispatch in cipher; and im. mediately the children of one of the schools of that place ran to every part of the town, and started all the church bells to ring. ing. The whole country was in a state of expectancy, and when the neighboring towns heard the bells of Brookline pealing, they all began to ring their own, so that, almost before the intelligence could be confirmed, it had spread throughout eastern Massachusetts.]

On wings of lightning the message came

To Brookline town, and it spread like flame

That April morning; for, two by two,

Over the village the children flew,

And set the bells in the belfrys tall

Rocking, and swinging, and ringing all;

And all the people, "with one accord,"

Halted, and hearkened, and praised the Lord,

As, speeding over the hills and dells,

The glad sound went of the Brookline bells!

And other bells, in the hamlets near,
Clamored, and echoed the music clear;
And cities heard, and a wide land knew
The import well of the strange ado.
It meant that down where the armies lay
At Appomattox, that famous day,
The veteran leaders, Grant and Lee,
Had parleyed under the apple-tree,
And signed the treaty that ushered in
Repose and safety where strife had been.

The clang and clamor—the sounds that rolled
From the vibrant bells of Brookline told
The march was ended, the vigil done,
The last shot sped from the smoking gun;
That the grim, long lines of blue and gray,
Like ghostly armies, would melt away,
And never again embattled stand,
In civil conflict, in all the land;
And the starry flag alone should be
The nation's emblem from sea to sea.

Like a dream-wraith fades and disappears
The cloud that darkened the battle-years;

Idle and useless, the bayonets rust;
The cannon are silent, and covered with dust;
The shot-torn banners in sleep are furled,
And Peace, like a zodiac, belts the world.
But long will the glad remembrance stay
Of all that happened that April day—
While Song rehearses, and History tells,
How the children rang the Brookline bells.

TO MINNIE.

My "remembrance," gentle girl?
    Scarce you need to ask it,
Since your friendship is the pearl
    Of my jewel-casket.

Changeless as the minted gold
    Of the yellow guinea
Is the tender thought I hold,
    Evermore, of Minnie.

THE ROSE SHE WORE.

The rose she wore upon her breast,—·
Though "charming, quite!" the maid confessed,
　Could scarce her lovliness enhance;
　It had a name that came from France—
It was the flower she loves the best.

I bought the prize at her behest;
'Twas costlier than I had guessed;
　I found it by the merest chance—
　　The rose she wore.

So, I observed with little zest,
When all the viols were at rest,
　As she and Albert quit the dance,
　And stood, exchanging glance for glance,
How that sweet flower was crushed, and pressed,—
　　The rose she wore.

THE BETTER DAY.

Above the far horizon rim,
  The east is tinged with gray;
'Tis coming, though its light be dim—
  The better day!

'Twill come in triumph when it comes,
  Howe'er it hastes, or lags;
But not with trumpets, nor with drums,
  Nor battle flags.

For war, and sounds of war, shall cease—
  The banners will be furled,
And liberty prevail, and peace,
  In all the world.

In that millennial, glorious time
  There'll be no poverty;
And ignorance shall be a crime
  By law's decree.

And every man, at every turn,
  Shall garner in the sweets,
And eat the bread he earns, and earn
  The bread he eats.

And none his neighbor's name shall speak
  To blacken and defame;
The strong shall guard and shield the weak
  From wrong and blame.

We'll little heed an outworn creed,
  But try the better plan
Of love, in thought, and word, and deed,
  To God and man.

And full-orbed Truth all souls shall draw,
  Like some great central sun,
And Right be one with Might,—and Law,
  And Justice, one.

The good, the true, the wise, the great,
  All hail its herald ray;
'Tis coming soon, in glorious state—
  The better day!

AN IDYL.

Summer, with blazon of gold, glory of leaf and of
blossom!
Under an amethyst sky, under gray clouds as they
pass!
Shimmers the lake in the sun—white lilies float on its
bosom,
Blithe bees hum in the fields, the crickets chirp in the
grass!

Loud is the bobolink's song, pipe the brown quail and
the plover,
Meadow-larks sing as they soar high o'er the verdurous
hills!
Song, and the joy of song, till the cup of the world runs
over
Brimmed with a tangle of tunes, pulsing with quavers
and trills!

Out from the maple shadows the sounds of mirth and
　　laughter　　　　　　　　　　　　　　　　　　·
Float on the odorous breeze, from the children at their
　　play,—
Jubilant shouts and greetings, and the echoes follow
　　after,
Over the valleys and fields, and over the hills away!

Joy is a sweet contagion—glad is the soul of the comer,
　　Here in a garden of sweets, here in an Eden of song;
As, seeking its solstice, the high-tide of life and of summer
　　Rises, and rolls through the land, rises and bears him
　　　along!

CHILD-QUESTIONINGS.

My little, orphaned niece, upon my knee,
  Plied me with childish questions, new and strange,
  In eager tone. Some were beyond the range
Of all my power to answer; two or three
Touched and involved that brooding mystery
  Which we call Death, the while her soft, blue eyes
  Grew weary—waiting my delayed replies—
In the dim twilight, by the summer sea.

"Dear uncle! Why did my sweet mother die,
  And go to heaven? Is heaven beyond that star?
  And can wee Carrie ever go so far
To meet her? Did God want her in the sky
  To tend my baby brother?" Then the deep
  Night shadows held us,—and she fell asleep.

THE LADY MOON.

The lady moon, a goddess bright,
With shoulders gleaming bare and white,
 And stately head in rev'ry bowed,
 Leans from her balcony of cloud
In the blue palace of the night.

Down peering from her queenly height,
She pours her soft, refulgent light
 Upon a merry-making crowd—
     The lady moon!

Apart, a maid and lover-wight,
Their troth with eager tremblings plight,—
 Lips meet, and solemn vows are vowed
 The while, serenely fair and proud,
Smiles sweet approval of the sight—
     The lady moon!

DESTINY.

A wise old mother is Nature,—
    She guideth her childrens' feet
In many a flowery pathway;
    And her strong life-currents beat,
Sometimes in intricate channels—
    As a mountain stream may run—
But ever her purpose triumphs,
    And ever the goal is won.
Her eyes are the eyes of Argus,
    And she utters her decree:
The brook shall come to the river,
    And the river shall reach the sea.

We have failed to read the riddle
    Of the impulse and desire,
That burn in the soul of being,
    Like the sun's great heart of fire,
Impelling the bird, storm-drifted,
    To come to its sheltered nest,

And the mother to bring her baby

The warmth of her shielding breast;

And the blossom to yield its honey

As the spoil of the bandit bee,—

While the brook goes down to the river

And the river reaches the sea.

But whatsoever we name it—

Be it Destiny, or Fate—

It leads the prince to his kingdom,

The king to his palace gate;

The lover shall taste the kisses

That grow on the maiden's lips;

And safe, in the land-locked harbor,

Shall be moored the wand'ring ships;

And the soul shall gain its heaven—

Where the white-robed angels be—

And the brook shall blend with the river

And the river shall wed the sea.

THE IDEAL FARMER.

The Farmer is the lord of lands,
  The birth-right baron of the soil,
  Although the callous-badge of toil
He wears upon his brawny hands.
Woods, fields and streams, are his demesne,
  The open sky his temple-dome,—
  The altar of his love the home
Where rules the priestess and the queen.

Like all of Nature's worshippers,
  He finds her treasures at his feet,
  And feels her warm life-pulses beat,
And makes his life a part of her's.
As Dawn unbars the gates of day,
  To ope the highway of the king,
  He wakens when the sparrows sing,
And rises with the robin's lay.

He traces in the mellow mold,

Where'er his gleaming plowshare runs

Dark lines for summer rains and suns

To print in characters of gold.

His wheat-fields glow like skies of morn,

And pasture-lands, and meadows green,

And fruitful orchards intervene,

Encircled by the bannered corn.

He watches, as the days go by—

Like grenadiers in single file—

The blossoms blow, the valleys smile;

Or notes the tumult of the sky,—

The lightning trim with fiery braid

The foldings of a mantle-cloud,

And thunders rolling far and loud,

Like echoes of a cannonade.

With rosy health, and wealth increased,

The fairest fruits before him spread,

He sits at table at the head,—

The proud Macgregor of the feast.

Good genii for him conspire

To foil the troubles that annoy,

And press the wine of every joy

Into the cup of his desire.

The pent up dwellers in the town—
That theater of petty strife—
Know little how his larger life
Keeps many a brood of follies down.
And so I hold, and justly call
This sturdy, independent man
The foremost in the social plan—
The helper, and the hope of all.

THE OLD AND THE NEW.

Out in the winter midnight,—
  Out in the darkness and cold,
Lieth a fallen monarch,—
  Wrinkled, and hoary, and old;
Broken his scepter lieth,
  His jeweled crown below,
And his beard doth rest
On his pulseless breast
  Like a drift of norland snow!

Scarce had the Christmas holly,
  Woven into his crown,
Twined with mistletoe, faded,
  Even a leaf, into brown,—
Scarce were the Christmas anthems,
  Matins, and vespers, sung,
Till through wood and dell,
Like a deep-toned bell,
  His knell by the winds was rung!

Spite of the tricks he played us,—
  On the ocean and the land—
Kind was he as a father,
  And he led us by the hand.
Ever bounty and blessing,
  Swept along in his train,
And his golden sheaves,
In the harvest eves,
  Filled many a loaded wain.

So, lightly weighing our sorrows,
  And ever recalli ng our joys,
Holding our moody spirits
  In quiet equipoise,—
Doing with manly courage
  Whatever we find to do,
We bury the Old
In the damp, dark mould,
  And joyfully hail the New!

THANKSGIVING.

The golden glow of autumn-time
  Hath faded like an ember,
And on the dreary landscape lies
  The first flakes of November;
Chill blows the wind through woods discrowned
  Of all their leafy glory,
As thus the seasons in their round
  Repeat the endless story!

The earth hath yielded up her fruits
  To bless the farmer's labors,
And peace and plenty crown the lives
  Of cheery friends and neighbors;
In fertile vales, on prairies broad,
  In homes by lake and river,
Ten thousand thousand hearts unite
  bless the Gracious Giver.

Thanksgiving for the harvest full,
  The orchards' mellow treasures,
The purple grapes, the golden corn,
  And all the joys and pleasures,
And bounties rich and manifold,
  That make life worth the living,—
For these, alike, the young and old,
  Join in a glad thanksgiving.

The kindly pair, whose weight of years
  With frosty locks hath crowned them;
Are seated at the festal board
  With all their children round them,
The father giveth fervent thanks
  In homely phrase and diction,
And stretches forth his aged hands
  In holy benediction.

Thus friends, long sundered, re-unite,
  Recount each joy and pleasure—
The annals of the fading past—
  And fill again the measure
Of youth, and healthful joyousness,
  As in the glad time olden,
When life was new, and skies were blue,
  And all the days were golden.

Thanks to the Pilgrim Fathers, then,
  Whose little goodly leaven
Works out through all the buried years
  This sweet foretaste of heaven.
And to the Lord, whose bounteous gifts
  Make life well worth the living,—
Who dwells above, whose name is Love—
  Be evermore thanksgiving!

THE PRESIDENT LIVES.

[These lines were written in Washington, D. C., July 25th, 1881, when President Garfield's physicians had just posted a bulletin announcing that the wounded man would recover from the murderous shot fired by Guiteau—a prediction that sadly failed of fulfillment.]

"Io Triumphe!"—at last!

Joyful, thrice joyful the sound!

Speeding the wide world around,

Swifter than wing of the blast!

Healing, and solace, it gives—

Rolls the dark shadow away—

Murder is robbed of its prey—

Lo! the good President lives!

Patience, that will not complain—

Marvellous courage, and strength,

Slowly emerging at length

From the red furnace of Pain!

Holding all hearts in his hand,
　　Fused into one in this hour,
　　Faction is shorn of its power—
Bitterness dumb in the land!

Fan him, all life-giving airs—
　　Make the quick fever-pulse calm;
　　Bring to him healing and balm—
More than we ask in our prayers!

Love hath no chaplet to give,
　　Richer than that on his brow;
　　Long may he wear it, as now—
Long may the President live!

HESPERUS.

His silver lamp fair Hesper lights,
  Above the mountain's crest;
No more the fierce tornado smites
With heavy hand the rocky heights,—
  The winds are lulled to rest.

The bright lake, like a beauteous child,
  Sleeps by the autumn wood;
No foot disturbs the dead leaves piled,—
No sound in all the forest wild
  To break the solitude,

Save, from the foot of yonder hill,
  Where vines and willows throng,
The drowsy tinkle of a rill,
And one lone, homeless whip-poor-will
  Singing her evening song.

Oh! that our lives, like this sweet hour,
  Might glide serenely by,
Without a cloud of ill to lower,
And dim the light, or mar the power
  Of Hope's bright star on high!

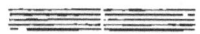

COMPANIONSHIP.

In quiet mountain valleys, miles between,
  Two little brooks welled up, the rocks among,
  And down their narrow channels danced; and sung
Their liquid songs; and flashed their silv'ry sheen,
In the unshaded spots of forests green,
  Till on a shelving ledge their waters hung
  One little moment, tremulous,—then flung
Them o'er the brink into a pool serene,
Wherein they met and mingled—happy streams!
  Two shining currents braided into one!
    So, in our lives, two comrade-spirits blend;
And sweet as fairy music heard in dreams,
  Is Love's triumphant song, the while they run
    The earthly race,—companions to the end.

OCTOBER.

Full wealth of pleasing sights
October brings us—rare delights
Of golden days, and moon-bright, silver nights.

The very air is wine,
And cordial, in its crystalline,
Cool sweetness, and we drink the nectar fine.

Some small, white flowers—the pledge
Of the dead Summer—star the edge
Of the wide field's embroidery of hedge.

The mountains wear their hoods
Of cloud with softer grace; there broods
A royal splendor over all the woods.

Leaves, red as sunset skies,—
Leaves, opulent with Tyrian dyes,
Or gold, or brown, a glory and surprise!

And scarlet berries shine;
And wild grapes, filled with ruddy wine,
Are meshed and held in tangled nets of vine.

Some migrant birds we know,
Whose notes in rippling music flow,
Are heard no more.   Ah! whither did they go?

Perhaps in far-off isles
Of Indian seas, where summer smiles,
Each song we love some weary heart beguiles.

Yet, the brown quail is here,
Piping, in treble, full and clear,
His song of home, and sweet content, and cheer.

The red-wing spreads his wings
Above the ripening corn, and sings—
Nor sweeter notes leaped from Apollo's strings.

And, shrill, the noisy jay,
A blue-coat cynic, day by day,
Scolds in the walnut tree across the way.

He scolds because, perchance,
He sees the darker days advance,
When Winter comes to couch a frosty lance;

Because the forest's crown
Of splendid leafage, drifting down,
Will leave his realm a landscape, bare and brown.

So moves the painted show—
Mirage of Summer! till the glow
Of Autumn dies, amid the falling snow!

THE OPTIMIST.

As oft the darkest pool reflects, at night,
  The everlasting stars that fill the sky,
  And we, beholding, almost deem they lie
Like orient jewels, scintillant, and bright,
Upon its bosom,—so Heaven's kindly light
  Is mirrored in the soul that you and I,
  Perchance, in our intolerance, pass by
As sordid, base, and unregenerate quite.

I hold the concept false—that this fair earth
  Whirls madly onward in a dance of death;
    Nay, every soul some germ of good enspheres,
Which God, himself, shall quicken into birth—
  Despite our narrow creed, and shibboleth—
    And it shall blossom through the endless years!

WINTER BIRDS.

Fair is the sky, for the cloud-rack is lifted,—
    Bright will the day be, though dark was the morn;
Warm was the morn, but the strong wind has shifted
    Into the north—where the blizzards are born.
White coward mercury goes down to zero,—
    Darting about flies a veteran jay,
Braving the breeze, like a blue-coated hero,—
    Seeking his supper, I venture to say.

Neighbors pass hurriedly, mantled and muffled—
    Great coats, and seal-skins, to keep out the storm—
Plump little quail, with their plumage beruffled,
    Search in the hedge for a nook that is warm,
That latest blast from the boreal bellows,
    Drifted some snow-birds the garden below;
Always their coming, the wise-acres tell us,
    Tokens cold weather, and flurries of snow.

Warm sheltered corners the cattle have chosen, --
Shivers the pine in its evergreen leaves;
Pools by the roadside in wrinkles are frozen,—
Bayonet icicles hang from the eaves.
Five English sparrows, defying the weather,
There in the pathway a conference hold;
Ho! merry midgets in doublets of feathers!
Why do you rally out there in the cold?

Little you care for the riot and rattle,—
Little you heed,—let the mercury fall!
Brave little fighters, go on with your battle—
Here is a friend who will welcome you all!
Fly to my window,—I'll feed every comer,—
Hail to the comrades that constancy show
Loving and loyal, in winter and summer,—
With us, alike, in the heat and snow!

THE SPANISH LOVE SONG.

Silver star! that shines on high
In the blue Castilian sky,
Dost thou in my lady's breast
Waken love-thoughts, unconfessed?

Happy bird! that sings for me
In yon blooming almond tree,
Thou hast hovered o'er her head;
Tell me what her sweet lips said!

Gipsy breeze! that strays at will
In the gardens of Seville,
Thou hast kissed her snowy brow;
Doth a shadow cloud it now?

Star! that through her lattice beams,
Bird! whose music threads her dreams,
Breeze! that kissed her tenderly,
Bring swift answer unto me!

MORNING HYMN.

To whom O Lord! if not to Thee,
   Shall song of praise ascend?
Before what throne but Thine shall knee
   Of erring mortal bend?

For all thy mercies, gracious King,
   In gratitude I raise
My voice in prayer, and loudly sing
   My hymn of joy and praise.

Thy smile hath made this radiant morn—
   Thy breath hath blown away
The stormy clouds of darkness born
   That veiled the rising day,

My morn of life was fair and bright,
   Its noon unclouded shines;
Do thou my footsteps guide aright
   Until the day declines.

And when the sun shall sink and hide,
   Within the shadows deep,
Let Thy sweet peace with me abide—
   Give Thy beloved sleep!

THE PIONEERS.

These are the heroes who triumphed o'er fate;
These are the toilers who moulded a state;
These are the soldiers who laughed at defeat;
This is the army that would not retreat!
These are the sturdy crusaders, and strong,
Worthy of places in story and song;
These the "Old Settlers" who came to the West
Long years ago. Let us give them the best
Of the good gifts which our hands may bestow
In the rich realm where the broad rivers flow—
Honor and cherish each name that appears
On the grand roll of the brave pioneers.

www.ingramcontent.com/pod-product-compliance
Lightning Source LLC
Chambersburg PA
CBHW020752020726
47495CB00008B/2393